The Social Media Massacre:

The Lost Scripts

By Ron Purtee

For Mom

Table of Contents

Introduction

It took me a while to realize what I should write for an introduction to this collection. I didn't want to make it seem like these are the lost tomes that have been missing for years, and if you don't read them, then your life will be empty… but these are lost tomes that have been missing for years, and your life will be empty if you don't read them.

I remember when I made the first incarnation of "The Social Media Massacre," it was ultimately out of simplicity. Setting up a webcam and shooting someone talking is probably the easiest and least visually pleasing thing you can do, but people seemed to like it. I don't know whether it was the performance by Charlie Bussian, or the overall tone of the piece, but here we are, 10+ years later, with a collection of unmade scripts from "The Social Media Massacre."

They were never made for one reason or another, and to be completely honest, I have always wanted to put out something like this, with things that I am never going to finish. Sure, there are other scripts that I haven't made and probably never will, but that is for another collection.

In this one, you will find rewrites of already filmed installments, and scripts that I tried to make forever with no luck. So, I thank you, Gentle Reader, for picking up this small collection of "Social Media Massacre" scripts that have been lost to time.

I hope you enjoy!

—Ron Purtee

Beta Testing

This is one of those scripts that I wrote during my "let's be as violent as possible" phase because I hadn't really discovered what it meant to be subtle, and this was very early in my career as a filmmaker.

At one point, we had four different people play the two roles in this script. We didn't make it due to money, time, and other issues with the universe playing games with the production, but I had to get this out, and this seems to be the only way to do it.

This script is about how far people will go to win … and to do it with a little style!

INT. LIVING ROOM - NIGHT

CHAD is sitting at his laptop. The view is from the webcam attached to the computer. He has a big grin on his face.

                CHAD
     No, I see what you mean;
     this is just awesome.
     It's best of the other
     two...

CHAD leans back in his chair and stretches. When he brings his arms down, a WOMAN comes from behind and slams his head into the table. He is groggy as the WOMAN binds his hands and places tape over his mouth. The WOMAN wipes her brow and fixes her hair.

                WOMAN
     There, that's much
     better. Screaming
     always gives me a
     headache.

She looks at the computer monitor as CHAD struggles to break free.

                WOMAN

Oh, Chad, that's just not good. I was hoping that I would have gotten here before you tried it out.
                    WOMAN (CONT.)
Then I could have just warned you, but you had to go and log on. Now, well, now I have to eliminate the problem.

CHAD is still struggling, trying to speak through the tape.

                    WOMAN
What's that? Oh, you wanna know what this is about. Well, that's totally understandable, and I assure you that it's nothing personal. You see, you decided to beta test this new piece of software that everyone wants, and my employer is not too happy about that. You see, the more people who don't use this software, who are SCARED to use this software, the more

people   stay   with   my
employer.

The WOMAN looks around the house.

                    WOMAN
Nice place you got here.

                    WOMAN (CONT.)
Got a real homey feel to
it. That the kitchen? I'm

on my feet all day; I'm
just going to make a
sandwich. You mind?

CHAD just struggles and groans.

                    WOMAN
Good.

The WOMAN walks offscreen. CHAD
notices that he left his webcam on.
He starts to groan words to anyone
who may be watching.

                    CHAD
          (through the tape)
Help me! Somebody PLEASE
help me!

                    WOMAN (O.S.)
Did you say something?

CHAD stifles himself.

               WOMAN (O.S.)
    I didn't think so. Say,
    you got any mayo?

CHAD struggles in the chair some
more.
The WOMAN walks back into the frame
of the webcam, licking her fingers.

               WOMAN
    Oh, that hit the spot.
    Would have been good if
    there had been some
    mayo...

The WOMAN sneezes.

               WOMAN
    Oh man, Chad you're
    holding out on me. You
    have a cat, don't you?
    Where is that little
    fucker?

The WOMAN leaves the view again. You
can hear her banging things around,
and a cat screaming.

               WOMAN (O.S.)
    Get the fuck over here,
    you son of a bitch!

There is a loud bang, and then
silence. The WOMAN comes walking
back into frame, cleaning her knife.
She leans in close to CHAD.

                    WOMAN
          Okay there, tough guy.

                    WOMAN (CONT.)
          It's time to get down to
          business. Because you
          played Captain Curious,

          you can't keep living,

          but don't think that I'm

          a heartless bitch. I'm
          going to give you an
          option: the boom...

The WOMAN pulls out a gun and places
it in front of CHAD.

                    WOMAN
          ...or the blade.

The WOMAN looks rather intently at
the knife.

                    WOMAN
          Well, what'll it be?

CHAD continues to struggle to break free from his bindings.

                    WOMAN
          Oh, to hell with it.

The WOMAN slices CHAD'S throat, and blood oozes out. She cleans off her blade and walks away. CHAD is still making a very annoying gurgling sound, as blood continues to ooze out.

                    WOMAN (O.S.)
          Fuck.   This   always
          happens.

We hear the click of a hammer, and the gun goes off as CHAD falls out of frame of the webcam.

                              CUT TO BLACK

I Started a Joke

This is one of the weirder ones, because at the end of the day, it's not 100% social media. I saw so many people doing ridiculous things online that I thought, "Why not someone faking their death online?" It's not incredibly farfetched.

What's different about this is that when you summon Death—even if you are joking—sometimes, Death comes for you.

The character of Death was supposed to be inspired by Julian Beck's performance as Kane in **Poltergeist 2**, so you can see where I was going with this.

INT. LYLA'S HOUSE - DAY

LYLA sits in front of the webcam on her computer. We see her the same way that someone watching her on the internet would be. She is growing increasingly upset as she films, on the verge of tears.

                    LYLA
          This video has been a
          long time coming. I
          realized that I need to
          make this, so I can tell
          you all at once. (pause)
          I'm dying.

LYLA starts to break up. A few tears leave her eyes.

                    LYLA
          As some of you know, I
          had a nasty infection,
          and the doctors... well,

          they couldn't't treat it,
          and now I am dying.

LYLA is full-on crying now. She breaks for a moment to wipe the tears away.

                    LYLA

There is another reason I'm making this video.

                    LYLA (CONT.)
A few years ago, there was a settlement that I was involved in. I didn't say anything to anyone because it involved a very embarrassing moment in my life. So, I have been sitting on A LOT of money all this time. Spending it felt dirty to me. Since I don't have any real family to speak of, this is what I am doing. Whoever wants it can have it. Plain and simple. So, here it is. There are 3.4 million dollars in—

The webcam shuts off. LYLA leans back and laughs, wiping the fake tears from her eyes.

                    LYLA
Oh, shit. That was hilarious. These morons are gonna be scrambling to find out where all this money is, and I'm

                    going to sit back and
                    laugh. Lyla, you are a
                    genius, you know that?

                         LYLA (CONT.)
                    Yes, Lyla, I have
                    recently been made aware
                    of this fact.

LYLA gets up, turns on the stereo,
and starts to dance around, very
proud of herself.

EXT. SIDEWALK - DAY

We see a pair of feet walking down
the sidewalk.

INT. LYLA'S HOUSE - DAY

LYLA is still dancing to the music,
using a hairbrush as a microphone.

EXT. FRONT OF LYLA'S HOUSE - DAY

A hand reaches out and knocks on the
door a few times.

INT. LYLA'S HOUSE - DAY

LYLA is still dancing around and
singing along to the music.

EXT. FRONT OF LYLA'S HOUSE - DAY

The same hand rings the doorbell a few times.

INT. LYLA'S HOUSE - DAY

LYLA hears the bell, turns off her music, and goes to the door. She opens it, and an old MAN, holding his hat and wearing a black suit, lifts his head with a big smile.

> MAN
> Yes, hello, my child. I was wondering if I could come in and have a word with you.

> LYLA
> Yeah, I'm kinda busy, and I couldn't really care less about AARP.

> MAN
> Well, I really think that it's in your best interest to allow me to come in and have a brief but very enlightening conversation with you.

                    LYLA
          Go to Hell, Grandpa.

LYLA slams the door in the MAN'S
face.

                    MAN
          (sighs) They always do
          this. I'd rather it be
          done   without   the
          theatrics, but so be it.

INT. LYLA'S HOUSE - DAY

A shot of the front door. There is
no one there. Suddenly, the MAN
appears out of nowhere, still
seemingly very docile.

                    MAN
          Lyla. Young lady, we
          REALLY need to talk.

LYLA freaks out that the MAN is in
the house. She runs to the kitchen,
reaches into the drawer, and pulls
out a gun. She aims it at the MAN
very uneasily.

                    LYLA

I don't know who you are,
but you picked the wrong
day, motherfucker.

She lets off a few rounds, and they
do nothing to the MAN. LYLA stands
there in shock.

                    MAN
          Tsk, tsk. I hate having
          to do this the hard way,
          but...

The MAN flips his hand, and the gun
flies out of LYLA'S hand. He puts
out his hand and draws LYLA towards
him. He wraps his hand around her
throat.   LYLA   begins   to   cry
hysterically.

                    LYLA
          WHAT   THE   HELL   DO   YOU
          WANT?

                    MAN
          You   told   the   world   you
          are dying.

                    LYLA
          It   was   a   joke.   JUST   A
          JOKE!

The MAN starts to lift LYLA into the air by her neck.

                    MAN
     Regardless of your sick
     sense of humor, the
     world has now been led
     to believe that you are
     not long for this world.
     Because of that, I am
     here to collect.
                    MAN (CONT.)
     You thought of life as a
     joke? Well, I am here to
     deliver the punchline,
     young lady.

The MAN snaps her neck with his hand and allows her body to fall to the floor.

We slowly pull back on her dead body, and then fade to the MAN putting his hat on and walking down the street.

                              FADE TO BLACK

Ride

This one was written a little more recently than the others.

As a society, we think that ridesharing is so safe, and there is a paper trail of when we get into the car, where we are going, and who is taking us there. We rely so much on trust when we pay someone to take us from Place A to Place B, but no matter how much stock we into a digital paper trail, some people just don't care.

That is where **Ride** comes into play.

So, the next time you order a car to take you home after a long night, make sure you get into the right one.

EXT. SIDE OF THE ROAD - NIGHT

BRIAN stands on the side of the road. He looks impatient. He checks his watch and grows more impatient. He looks up and down the street before pulling out his phone and tapping on it a few times. He puts it away, and a car pulls up.

He walks up to the passenger-side door, and the window slowly descends. It's dark, and we can't really make out who is in the driver's seat.

                    BRIAN
          I'm Brian. You Eddie?

                    EDDIE (O.S.)
          Yeah. Get in.

BRIAN seems a bit apprehensive, but he checks his watch and gets in the car anyway.

INT. CAR - NIGHT

The light is so dim that we can only really see BRIAN'S face. EDDIE is shrouded in darkness. You can really only make out the back of his head.

                    BRIAN

So, I'm new to this whole
app-taxi thing, but you
were a few minutes late.
Figured that was Rule
Number One.

EDDIE says nothing.

                    BRIAN

You know where I'm going,
right? Just about half a
mile up the road. I
could have walked, but I
got a bad back, so I
don't wanna aggravate
that.

EDDIE remains silent.

                    BRIAN
Not a very talkative
guy, are ya? Might make
more in the way of tips
if you engaged in human
interaction.

EDDIE is still silent. Now, so is
BRIAN.

The rest of the short ride is very awkward.

The car comes to a stop. BRIAN pulls out his phone and taps on it a few times.

                BRIAN
     There, you're paid. In
     the future, I'd think
     that if you wanted a
     tip, you'd be a little
     more personable—

BRIAN'S door flies open, and a pair of arms yanks him out. There are sounds of a struggle, and finally a long, fatal scream.

A WOMAN leans her head into the car and tosses EDDIE an envelope.

                WOMAN
     Good job. Keep 'em
     coming.

She shuts the door, and EDDIE takes off down the road.

                         FADE TO BLACK

Face Time

This story was based on something that Derrick Carey and I spoke about over Facebook Messenger. I remember thinking about casting myself in this one because it is such a simple script with such a harsh and abrupt ending.

It really puts a spotlight on how technology has made it easier to communicate face to face, but that isn't always the best thing; sometimes, it can be fatal.

This may be one of the ones I really regret not making because it could have been so simple; yet here we are. So, enjoy!

INT/EXT

RICK is walking outside on his phone, using the Face Time app.

AMY is at home, sitting in a chair, using the same app.

                RICK
     This is the coolest
     thing. Totally worth the
     wait in line at the
     store.

                AMY
     Isn't this kind of
     pointless? I mean, if
     you want to see me, then
     can't you just come home?

                RICK
     It's the future! Either
     get onboard or be left
     behind, honey!

                AMY
     Well, can I at least
     talk to Greggy? I'm sure
     he thinks this is great.

RICK pauses for a moment and looks down in shame.

                    AMY
What? What aren't you
telling me?

                    RICK
I forgot to pick him up
from school.

                    AMY
What are you talking
about?! Tell me you are
joking!

                    RICK
No. I totally forgot to
get him.

                    AMY
What the hell were you
so busy doing?

                    RICK
I was at the store,
getting this thing, and
I kind of lost track of
time.

                    AMY
A fucking phone was more
important than your own
son?! He's only five

years old! Who knows what the hell could have happened to him?!

                    RICK

You don't have to yell; I know I fucked up. I'll fix it. I promise. I'm on my way to get him right now. I feel so damn bad about this.

                    AMY
Feel bad?! You better feel worse than bad, you son of a bitch! In all the seven years we have been together, you have never fucked up this bad!

                    RICK

I know! You don't have to yell at me! There is nothing I can say that will fix this. I'm on my way now to get him—

There is a loud screech of tires. RICK looks to his left, and everything goes crazy. It looks like the camera is flying through the

air, and it lands on its side. RICK
falls to the ground, his eyes still
wide open.

                AMY
     RICK?! RICK, WHAT THE
     FUCK IS GOING ON?!

We hear sirens in the background, as
AMY begins to sob uncontrollably.

                    CUT TO BLACK

A Hollywood Ending (Redux)

Once I realized how to make films and how to make things visually appealing, and once I had the facilities to get things made, I almost remade the original installment of "The Social Media Massacre." It would have been expanded, more than just a face in front of the camera, more than 1-2 actors, and—gasp!—actually leaving the living room!

This story is longer, and we follow Sam outside the house after the end of the original episode. We see that no matter how bad someone is, the best place to hide is in plain sight in "The Social Media Massacre."

INT. KITCHEN

SAM is sitting in front of the
camera.

                SAM
Hey, my name is Sam. I'm
30. I'm from the Midwest.
I'd say where, but let's
be honest; people either
forget about the Midwest
altogether or think all
the cities are the same.
So, I started
"vlogging." Seemed like
the hip thing to do and
far be it for me to
ignore a trend. A little
bit about myself: I'm a
web designer; I do a lot
of work from home,
through e-mail and such.
I do well, but it doesn't
exactly lend itself to
social interaction. I'm
not even sure if I have
the skills, anyway.

SAM rubs the back of his neck.

                SAM

I was always hoping that I could find someone, you know? Or even just something to complete me, make me whole.

SAM takes a drink from the glass next to him. He is getting more and more nervous as time ticks on.

                SAM
I did my share of dating recently. First, there was Hannah. We met on one of those dating sites — I forget which one — and we went out, and things went great. For a while, I thought I was out of my slump, and things were picking up for me. Then Hannah changed. She got weird, cold, almost dead inside.

INT. LIVING ROOM

A flash of HANNAH'S dead body propped up in a chair, like she is alive.

INT. KITCHEN

SAM rubs his face with his hands and
sighs.

           SAM
So, then there was Mary.

           SAM (CONT.)
I figured I fell off the
horse with Hannah; I had
to get back on. That's
what they say, right?
There was something
about her that I really
liked. Don't ask me what
it was, but I thought we
hit it off.

INT. LIVING ROOM

A flash of SAM hitting MARY with his
fist.

INT. KITCHEN

SAM rubs the hand that he hit MARY
with.

           SAM
I guess she wasn't as
virginal as I thought.
She was nothing like

that. I just wanted my happy ending. They make it seem so simple in movies and TV. I didn't want to be alone anymore. (beat) Then I went out one night, and I found the woman of my dreams.

                    SAM (CONT.)
She is ABSOLUTELY perfect. You have to meet her. She's here. Ang. Come here, hun! She's shy; I'll get her.

SAM gets up and walks out of frame. He comes back in, dragging ANGIE on the floor. He lifts her up and positions her on his lap, treating her almost like a puppet.

                    SAM
See! I told you she was perfect!

SAM brushes the hair away from her face and kisses her on the cheek.

                    SAM

We are gonna be together
forever, aren't we, baby?
Forever.

INT. BEDROOM - MORNING

SAM has just finished having "sex"
with ANGIE. He rolls off her and
sighs.

                    SAM
That was great, baby.

                    SAM (CONT.)
Really   felt   the
connection there but...
(beat) What do you mean,
you know where this is
going?   (beat)   Fine!
You're right. This isn't
going anywhere. (beat)
No, fuck you... and get
out of my bed!

SAM pushes ANGIE to the floor and
starts to tear up a little.

INT. BATHROOM

SAM is sitting on the edge of the
bathtub. Next to him is a full
garbage bag, and one that is about
half full. He is crying a little.

                    SAM

Why? Why couldn't you
love me? What's wrong
with me? Am I that bad?
Was it something I said?
Did? Didn't do? I just
wanted you to love me,
and you couldn't do
that. COULD YOU?! Well,
now we have a
predicament. I can't
leave you here.

                  SAM (CONT.)

I can't send you off with
your belongings into
that good night. Nope,
the trash bag it is.

SAM pulls ANGIE'S decapitated head
out of the blood-soaked bathtub. He
looks at it with tears in his eyes
and kisses her lovingly.

                    SAM

You broke my heart, you
fucking bitch.

SAM puts the head in the bag and
ties it up.

SAM looks in the mirror as he washes his hands. His facial expression is pure heartbreak and hate.

SAM pulls a large black garbage bag down the hallway. It is obviously very heavy and is giving him a hard time. He falls over while pulling it. He gets up and pulls it out the door.

EXT. SAM'S CAR - DAY

SAM opens the trunk and throws the large black garbage bag in.

EXT. ALLEYWAY - DAY

SAM deposits the large black bag into a dumpster. He brushes his hands off and walks away.

On his way to his car, he runs into JOAN.

                    JOAN
    Hey,   Sam.   It's   been
    forever.   High   school,
    right?

SAM is obviously very nervous after
what he's just done.

                SAM
     Yeah. Yeah, we had the
     same homeroom.

                JOAN
     That's right! This may be

     a little forward, but I'm
     not doing anything right
     now; do you wanna get
     some coffee?

                SAM
     Um...

He looks back at the dumpster.

                SAM
     Sure. Why not? Sounds
     like a date!

SAM puts his arm around JOAN, and
they walk away. As they are walking
away, SAM looks back at the camera
and winks. Freeze on that image as
the music comes up...

                    CUT TO BLACK

Afterword

I hope you enjoyed these scripts as much as my films, and as you read them, I hope you used your imagination to "watch" them as they were meant to be filmed. I hope they delighted you, terrified you, or creeped you out!

Who knows what the future holds for my filmmaking career? At the end of the day, I hope you keep coming back for more because, to quote Pinhead, "I have such sights to show you…!"

Acknowledgments

I want to thank my brother Kevin for putting up with me for his entire life—and mostly while trying to find these scripts after I'd gone through a couple of computers and was horrible at backing things up. We got this, bud!

I also want to thank my amazing editor, Abbey Decker, who really believed in this project and believes in me. I will now eat a pallet. She knows what I mean.

Finally, thank you, the viewer, the reader, the consumer of content. Without you, I would have no outlet for my madness. You are amazing!

Ron Purtee was born, raised, and still lives in Wisconsin.

He is feverishly working on his next project.

More Information

Other Works by Ron Purtee
Tales of Shock and Terror #1 (co-author) from
Cutthroat Comics

Coming Soon by Ron Purtee
I'll Be Right Behind You (short film)

Social Media
You can find Ron on most social media platforms as
@imuncleron

Website
www.uncleronsdrivein.com